The children were outside.
A hot air balloon went by.

Mrs May had a secret.
She told Wilf what it was.

She wanted to go in a balloon.

It was time to watch television.
The television went wrong.

'Oh no!' said Mrs May.

The photocopier went wrong.

'Oh blow!' said Mrs May.

The computer went wrong.

'Oh bother!' said Mrs May.

Wilf and Wilma came home.
They had a letter.

The school wanted money.
Wilf had an idea.

Everyone liked Wilf's idea.
'It's a good idea!' everyone said.

Everyone bought tickets.

Mrs May bought lots of tickets.

She wanted to go in the balloon.

Mrs May won the prize.
She won a ride in the balloon.

'Hooray!' said Wilf.

Mrs May went up in the balloon.
'Hooray,' shouted everyone.

'It's wonderful,' said Mrs May.

Mrs May saw the stream.
She saw the houses.

She looked down at the park.
She took this photograph.

The school made lots of money.
They bought lots of things.

Mrs May was pleased.
She gave Wilf a present.

'Thank you,' said Wilf.